# Contents

## CHAPTER ONE

# Good Things to Eat

Kalulu the rabbit was very wise. He knew that the best way to get good things to eat was to grow them.

One day, Kalulu decided to grow some pumpkins.

"Hello, Buru," he said to his friend, the elephant. "I am going to grow some pumpkins."

The elephant smiled a big smile. "I like pumpkins," he said.

"Then why don't you grow some?" asked Kalulu.

"I haven't got any seeds," replied the elephant.

"Oh, dear," said Kalulu. "You can have some of mine." So Kalulu gave half of his seeds to the elephant.

"Is that all you're going to give me?" asked Buru. "I want more seeds than that!"

"I'm sorry," said Kalulu. "This is all I have."

"I suppose it will have to do then," grumbled the elephant. "How do I plant them?"

"Come to my garden early in the morning," said the rabbit. "I will show you what to do."

The elephant went away, and Kalulu went to bed so that he would be ready to plant his seeds early in the morning.

## CHAPTER TWO

# Selfish Kalulu!

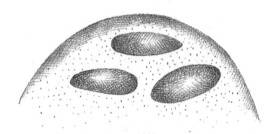

The next day, Kalulu got up bright and early. He carried his shiny new hoe to his garden. He hoed the ground until it was soft and crumbly, then he scooped the earth up into big mounds. In each mound, he planted three pumpkin seeds.

When the seeds were planted, Kalulu sprinkled them with water from the nearby river and covered them with banana leaves to shade them from the hot sun.

"There!" said the rabbit. "Finished at last!"

As soon as Kalulu said this, Buru the elephant appeared. He was grumbling about how early it was.

"Early!" said the rabbit. "It's not early! I've been up for hours. Look— I've finished planting my seeds."

Buru looked at the ground and saw the mounds of earth. "That's not fair!" he shouted. "You should have waited for me."

"Don't worry," said the rabbit. "I will still show you what to do. Did you bring your hoe?"

"No," said the elephant. "Yours is new and shiny. I want to use yours."

Kalulu did not like other people using his hoe. He was worried that it would get broken. "I'd rather you used your own hoe," he said.

The elephant was not happy. "You are very mean and selfish," he said. "You should be ashamed of yourself."

Kalulu felt very bad. "I'm sorry," he said. "Of course you can borrow my hoe. Here it is."

Kalulu handed the hoe to the elephant. He showed Buru how to hoe the ground and how to plant the seeds.

Buru waved the hoe around with his trunk. He stabbed at the ground.

"Not like that!" said Kalulu.

Buru threw the hoe down in a fit of temper. "It's too hard," said Buru. "You will have to hoe the ground for me."

The rabbit was hot and tired. He had been up since dawn and he wanted to go home and have some breakfast.

"No," he said. "I will not do it for you. You must do it yourself."

The elephant was very angry. "You are selfish!" he said. "I don't know why I bother being your friend!" Without another word, Buru took his seeds and stomped off to his own garden.

Kalulu watched him go.

## CHAPTER THREE

# Seven Times Three

Every day for a week, Kalulu watered his pumpkin seeds. He got up early in the morning and got water from the river. He sprinkled it onto the dry earth. Every day he shaded the mound of earth with fresh banana leaves. He knew that the seeds would not grow unless he took care of them.

"Are you taking good care of your seeds?"
Kalulu shouted to Buru when he saw him drinking at the river one morning.

The elephant hardly looked up. "They're fine," he mumbled.

"Good," said Kalulu. "I think mine will be coming up soon."

The elephant raised his head. "So will mine," he said.

Kalulu smiled and hopped back to his garden.

Kalulu looked at the mounds of earth. A tiny green seedling was pushing its way through the crumbly soil.

"My first pumpkin plant!" shouted Kalulu.

The rabbit was overjoyed. He sat by the mounds of earth all day and watched as the pumpkin seedlings broke through the ground, one by one. As the sun sank, Kalulu counted his beautiful pumpkin plants. Each mound had three fine, healthy seedlings, and there were seven mounds.

"Seven times three," said Kalulu. "That will be 21 pumpkins. What a feast I will be able to share with my friends!"

CHAPTER FOUR

# Bad Seed

The next morning, Kalulu hopped over to Buru's house. He knocked on the door. "Buru!" he shouted. "Are you home?"

There was no answer.

"Ah!" thought Kalulu. "Buru is probably in his garden watering his plants. I will go and see how he is doing."

Kalulu hopped around to Buru's garden.

"Oh, no!" he said aloud in a shocked voice.

There were no seedlings growing in Buru's garden. The soil was dry and cracked. It hadn't been watered or hoed in a very long time. The earth was badly scraped together in tiny piles and the seeds lay scattered on the top. The sun had scorched and burned them to a crisp.

"What a waste of seeds!" cried Kalulu. He looked at the poor, burned seeds and felt like crying.

Sadly, the rabbit started his journey back home. He found his beautiful shiny hoe abandoned in a ditch. The elephant had not even bothered to return it. He had left it lying in a pile of dirt and weeds.

When Kalulu was nearly home, he heard an angry, trumpeting noise.

"That sounds like Buru!" he thought.

He was right. It was Buru. He was standing in the middle of Kalulu's garden, stamping his big feet on the mounds of earth. The tiny pumpkin plants were being flattened.

"Stop!" shouted Kalulu. "What are you doing?"

"You cheated!" roared the elephant. "You gave me bad seeds and took all the good ones for yourself!"

"No, I didn't," cried Kalulu.

"Yes, you did," trumpeted the elephant. "Your seedlings have grown, and mine have not!" Buru's big feet hovered over another mound.

"Don't do that!" shouted Kalulu. "If you squash all the seedlings, there will be no pumpkins to eat at all."

Buru thought about this. He coughed politely and lowered his foot gently back to the ground.

"Oh, I am sorry," he said. "I don't know what came over me. I didn't mean any harm." Buru tried to straighten the squashed seedlings with his trunk.

17

"It's all right," said Kalulu. "I understand. You were disappointed that your seeds didn't grow."

"Yes," said the elephant. "But I am willing to forgive you for giving me bad seeds. We are friends after all." With a swing of his trunk, Buru walked away.

## CHAPTER FIVE

# Where Is Buru?

Days passed, and Kalulu did not see Buru. He heard from his other friends, Turtle, Jackal, and Warthog, that Buru had gone away to visit his aunt.

"I hope he'll be back in time to share the pumpkins," said Kalulu.

Kalulu's friends looked at the pumpkin plants. Buru had flattened nine of them. There were only 12 left.

Kalulu watered the 12 pumpkin plants. Every day they grew bigger and bigger.

One day, Kalulu saw white flowers on his pumpkins.

"Hooray!" said Kalulu. "When the flowers fall off, the ripe, juicy pumpkins will grow."

That is exactly what happened. The white flowers bloomed, then quickly fell to the ground. In their place grew beautiful big pumpkins.

Every day, Kalulu pinched and prodded the pumpkins. He wanted to know when they were ripe enough to eat. One morning, he decided that the biggest pumpkin was ready.

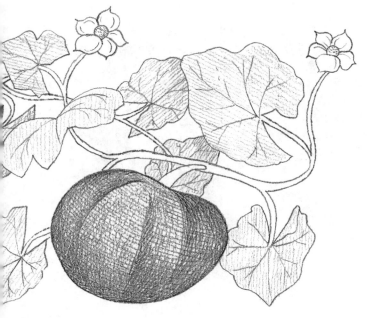

"I will pick it tomorrow," he thought. "But first I must invite all my friends to share the feast."

Kalulu visited Turtle, Jackal, and Warthog.

"Will you come and share breakfast with me in the morning?" he asked. "One of my pumpkins is ripe and juicy. It's ready to be picked."

Kalulu's friends agreed to come.

"Have you invited Buru?" they asked.

"Not yet," said Kalulu. "But I will."

Kalulu hopped around to the elephant's house. He knocked at the door. "Is anyone home?" he shouted. No one answered. "He must still be away," thought Kalulu.

Kalulu went home and got ready for his friends' visit the next morning. He watered the pumpkin one final time and went to sleep, dreaming of how wonderful it would taste.

## CHAPTER SIX

# My Beautiful Pumpkin!

The next morning, Kalulu got up very early. He hopped down to his garden. The sun was barely creeping over the horizon, and the whole garden was bathed in a strange orange glow.

Kalulu thought he saw a dark shadow creeping away from his garden, but he was too excited to worry about what it could be. He got his wheelbarrow from the shed and pushed it over toward the ripe pumpkin. He knew he would never be able to carry such a huge pumpkin in his tiny paws. He would heave it into the wheelbarrow and push it back home.

Rabbit looked at the pumpkin plant. He rubbed his eyes with his paws. He could not believe what he saw. The pumpkin was gone!

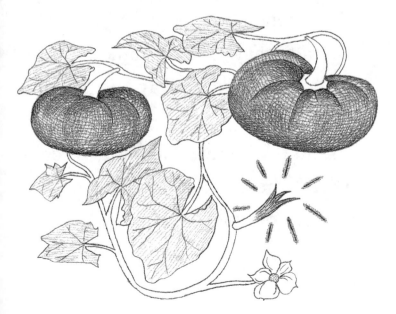

"Where is my beautiful, ripe pumpkin?" he cried.

Kalulu's friends came running to see what was the matter. "Someone has stolen your pumpkin!" they said.

Kalulu was very sad. He could not believe that anyone would take his pumpkin.

"Who would do such a thing?" he asked.

Everyone shook their heads. The only one they could think of was Buru, and he was away visiting his aunt.

"Never mind, Kalulu," said Turtle. "There are still lots of pumpkins left for you to eat."

Kalulu tried to smile. "You are right," he said. "I must not be sad.

Whoever took the pumpkin was probably very hungry. They are welcome to it. We will have a feast tomorrow when the next pumpkin is ripe."

Kalulu's friends agreed to come back the next morning. They all waved goodbye and went home.

## CHAPTER SEVEN

# Tusks and Trunks

Kalulu sat down to think. He tied a strip of banana leaf around his head to keep the sun off his brow. "I don't want another pumpkin to be stolen," he said aloud. "I must protect this one."

That night, Kalulu waited until it was dark. Then he went back to the garden, carrying his drum. He looked at the second pumpkin. It was now even bigger than the first one.

"I will scoop out the pumpkin and hide inside it," said Kalulu. "Then if anyone tries to steal my pumpkin, I will jump out and bang my drum. That will scare them away."

Kalulu scooped out the pumpkin and curled up inside it. He tried to stay awake, but it was hot and stuffy inside the pumpkin. Long before morning had come, he was fast asleep.

As the sun started to light the morning sky, Kalulu heard a noise. He jumped up and peeked out of the pumpkin. He saw a huge pair of white tusks and a long trunk curled around the pumpkin.

"Buru!" shouted Kalulu. But it was too late. Buru swallowed the pumpkin whole. Kalulu was still inside it!

## CHAPTER EIGHT

# The Beating Drum

Down, down inside the elephant's throat went Kalulu.

"Help!" he called. But no one could hear him. Kalulu and the pumpkin were deep inside Buru's stomach.

"Now, what will I do?" thought Kalulu. He looked at the drum that was still in his paws. "I know," he thought. "I will beat my drum."

So Kalulu beat his drum.

Buru heard a distant rat-a-tat-tat.
"Oh, no!" he trumpeted. "Someone
must have seen me come into the
garden. They are calling for help
with a drum. I had better run away."

So Buru ran. He ran and ran and ran. After he had run for a whole mile, the drum stopped beating.

"At last!" sighed the elephant. "I am safe." Buru sank to his knees and gasped for air.

But as soon as he had recovered his breath, the beating started again. This time it was louder. Rat-a-tat-tat! Rat-a-tat-tat!

Buru started to run again. He ran for three miles this time before the drum stopped beating.

"I must be safe now," gasped Buru.

But he was wrong. He could not run away from the beating drum because the drum was inside him.

Every time Buru stopped running, the drum started to beat again. And every time it started, it got louder and louder.

Kalulu hated being inside the elephant's stomach. He wanted to get out. He beat on his drum as hard as he could. RAT—A—TAT— TAT! RAT—A—TAT—TAT!

Buru ran and ran. Soon he was exhausted. He could not run another step. He sank to the ground and fell asleep with his mouth wide open.

Kalulu stopped beating the drum. He waited until Buru was fast asleep, then he crawled out of his open mouth.

"There!" said Kalulu. "That will teach Buru a lesson!"

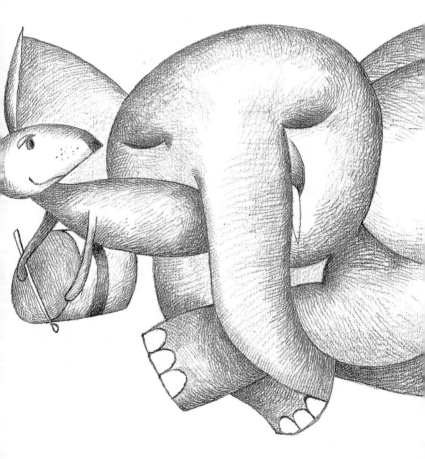

He was right. When Buru woke up, the first thing he said was, "I'll never steal another pumpkin as long as I live!"

Kalulu heard this and was glad. He crept out from behind the bushes where he had been hiding, and he hopped happily back home.

# Kalulu's Pumpkins

Retold by Amber Medcroft

Illustrated by Jiri Tibor Novak

Rigby